Those Cloaked in Purple

Dawn Blair

Cover and layout copyright © 2025 by Morning Sky Studios
Cover design by Dawn Blair/Morning Sky Studios
Cover art copyright © Sorrapong Apidech | Dreamstime.com, © Tomert | Dreamstime.com, © Imphilip | Dreamstime.com

Morning Sky Studios
PO Box 5422
Twin Falls, ID 83303
Visit us at www.morningskystudios.com

Also by Dawn Blair:

Dragons of Wellsdeep

Beat of the Drum

Stonecharmer

Stonecharmer

Stonebreaker

Stonesinger

Onesong

Palladium

Tangled Magic

Walk the Path

Sacred Knight

Quest for the Three Books

Manifest the Magic

To Birth a Destiny

Prince of the Ruined Land

The Missing Thread

Sword and Shield

The Loki Adventures

1-800-CallLoki (Omnibus of novellas 1-5)

1-800-IceBaby

Help Wanted, Call Loki

1-800-Lok8

Dressed to the 9's

Perfect 10

Wells of the Onesong

Fractured Echo

Fall's Confession

The Doorway Prince

Stardust

Mystery of the Stardust Monk

Alexander's Den

Other Short Stories

Hot Yoga

The Tales of Quanst the Mouse

A Doll in Solitary

Those Cloaked in Purple

Early morning light stretched into the stone castle's royal bedroom, along with the faintest stirring of a dewy breeze through the open balcony doors. Outside, a few thin clouds relaxed along the horizon, reflecting oranges and pinks to help chase away the pre-dawn grey. The sky was just starting to turn the lightest of blues.

Cirvel never tired of noticing how each beautiful day started in his mountain city of Gohaldinest. It seemed like the dark wood panels lining the room's interior walls to cut down the drafts coming into the room always reflected new colors each day. He loved each nuance of the world he'd come to call his home.

He currently stood on a short, wooden box and admired himself in the full-length oval mirror slightly tilted in its stand near the wood paneled wall across from the foot of his bed. A tailor – a short, wispy, and balding man with elegantly long fingers which Cirvel liked to watch as the man deftly made his stitches – worked at the bottom hem of the black robes, pinning the cloth in place. It would be so easy to use genie magic and just craft the cloth as Cirvel saw it in his mind, but anticipation of the final product made him willing to let the work be done by hand. It would be worth the wait.

Another curl of the morning breeze wafted through the open balcony doors. Flutterbirds played in the potted trees in both far corners of the balcony. He'd come to learn, in the short time he'd been on this planet, that flutterbirds had to keep their wings moving so that their hearts would beat. Stopping for too long meant that the tiny, colorful birds would die.

He couldn't imagine not being able to curl up at night with his love. That might make his heart stop beating. As if she could feel the swell of emotion that went through him, his beautiful wife, Treshauna, gave a soft moan and stretched in the silky sheets of their bed. The rustling of the sheets made him want to go to her. But that might annoy the tailor at his feet.

Not that he cared much. Cirvel could banish the man away with words or with a bare thought of his magic.

But these robes he was crafting for himself, he was doing for her, and he wanted to see her delight.

A soft knock tapped at the door before a servant entered with a plate of sliced pears. The servant kept his eyes down as he walked with the sound of a whisper across the room and set the plate on the table and disappeared just as quickly. Cirvel smelled the fragrance of the pears all the way across the room. He gave hope that it would be enough to wake Treshauna from her sleep.

He couldn't keep his eyes off his blonde love, her hair falling over pillow and blankets and even across her gentle face. The bedding nestled around her, revealing her wonderful curves. With the fruity scent enticing him, he wanted to go and breathe deeply of her skin. She always smelled like fruit and honey, and her hair was fragranced like sunshine.

He felt like the luckiest man alive.

"Do you wish the thread to be gold or silver? Or perhaps another color?" the tailor asked, breaking Cirvel from the spell of his thoughts. He could have cursed the man.

"Silver," he said. Though gold was the color of Treshauna's hair, he knew that if he had to look at gold threads every day after he eventually lost her, he'd go mad. Humans didn't live as long as genies, and, as such, he was destined to one day lose her. Besides, gold was the imprisonment of a genie. He had enough of the metal with his lamp and Treshauna's wavy hair. While being held captive to one of those was a pleasure, the other was a bane.

He heard the sheets rustle again as Treshauna moved between them. He knew how her body moved, especially between the silky layers of their bed, and he longed to join her as she gently roused herself for the day. But the tailor tugged on the cloth as he shoved a new pin in, and it brought Cirvel's attention down to the man at his feet.

"Cirvel, love, new royal robes? Why must you go with black?" Treshauna asked. Her words were long and drawn out by the sleepiness which still held her.

Cirvel raised his head, feeling himself jerk back slightly. He hadn't imagined that she'd be appalled by his choice. Rather, he thought she'd be delighted and supportive. "You don't like it?"

"I'm just saying, with Hazem training under me, I feel as if the color should be reserved for the Black Nights."

This was going to be a problem. Even before meeting her, he'd worn black. He felt comfortable in dark cloth. On the day they'd met, he'd been in a black cloak even under the desert sun. It wasn't a color reserved for only the Black Nights, though she'd often discouraged him from wearing it as if it were only for the master energy workers. He understood her point why the Black Nights needed to be garbed in somber colors, but on this world, it wouldn't matter. Black Nights wore black because life energy was often tainted and needed cleansed and cleared so it could return to the All. But here, on this world spun off from the Onesong, there was no return to the larger source in the universe. The energy they had was all they were ever going to get until this planet died or was somehow, miraculously, redeemed. It would be a good, long time before he allowed that to happen. The humans of this world deserved no salvation.

Unfortunately, that doomed his family as well.

So they would have to make do with what they had, and Cirvel knew his plans would have to last generations. Every thought he had needed to span into the future. That meant setting up strong traditions.

"Darling," Cirvel said smoothly and with a soft smile. He was going to once again have to enlighten her to the truth, and he didn't want to do it, but she needed to accept the fact. "You and Hazem are the last people who will ever be capable of being Black Nights on this world."

She looked sad, like he knew she would be. But it was true. Hazem was the last child she'd have, that they'd have together, so there'd be no more that could wield the abilities of the Black Nights like she did. It became a short heredity due to their planet being spun off the Onesong. When Hazem had children, there was a good chance his genie magic would diminish any Black Night abilities the young ones might have. When Treshauna and Hazem both perished from the world, and Cirvel knew they both would one day be gone from him, this world would never be able to support a Black Night ever again. He didn't want to tell her, but the black robes were his way of making sure that her and Hazem's lives would be memorialized for all time. He would wear black to honor her and he'd make sure that all following royalty would do the same.

"You realize that Kahlila will look horrible in black," Treshauna said.

He grinned, knowing how she was utterly lying. Their eldest daughter, Kahlila, was the spitting image of her mother. Lean, playful eyes, long and wavy blonde hair. Cirvel couldn't believe he was Kahlila's father and that he'd helped to bring such a lovely creature into this world. The thing with genie magic was, however, that it always was strongest in the first born when conceived in a mixed-race relationship.

He, himself, had been the first child of a mating between a human and a genie. Unlike most of the dragon born novihomidraks, he remembered his parents, and the knowledge hadn't made him insane. It had to have been his genie magic which protected his mind as he underwent the process to become one of the dragon's champions. In his case, no one knew what would happen if a nonhuman was chosen to become a novihomidrak. He'd been an experiment. He'd come through strong and become more powerful than he would have been otherwise allowed as a lower class, half-breed genie looked down on by others.

But Kahlila had surprised them both. She looked very much like her mother, but her genie magic was as powerful as Cirvel's. Hazem, on the other hand, looked like Cirvel, but had his mother's abilities.

For Treshauna to say that Kahlila would look horrible in black was her way of saying that she felt she looked terrible in black. That was simply a state that held no truth.

Treshauna rose naked from between the sheets. Cirvel watched her walk toward the pears and pick one up, but he noticed how the tailor at his feet tugged a little harder at the hem of the cloth to force his attention on his work. Cirvel didn't envy the man. It was far easier to watch Treshauna than to look away. Her curves were smooth and ample. Blonde hair tickled at her skin. Here, in the mountains, her skin had lost the light desert tan she'd had when they'd met. Now she was as truly white as a pearl. His lovely pearl.

As much as he wanted her gaze to slide sidelong to see if Cirvel was watching her, she didn't. She didn't need to. She probably read it in his energy and knew exactly what he was feeling, even the subconscious thoughts he didn't realize.

She turned when she picked up a piece of sliced pear and bit into it. Just watching her and still smelling the fruit, he could practically taste it himself. She caught a drip of the fruit's sweet juice on her finger and licked it off. Her eyes were closed, mouth slightly upturned. She was definitely feeling his emotions and loving every moment of it.

After a moment, she exhaled a long breath and

walked over to the wardrobe they shared. Doors open, she began to choose her clothes for the day.

A much more solid knock came to the door than the one from earlier when the servant had entered with the pears. There was barely a wait before the door was pounded again. Even the tailor had stopped working, and was prepared to get out of Cirvel's way should he step down from the box.

Treshauna was no longer trying to dress in a leisurely fashion, but Cirvel hurried her along with a wisp of magic as he said, "Come."

The door opened as Cirvel's magic completely clothed his wife, and a soldier entered. Whatever the soldier thought of Cirvel getting robes fitted for him by the tailor he hid completely as he saluted and began his reason for coming. "My lord, we believe there are Plenelian Death Rogues in the castle."

"Believe?" Cirvel asked. Belief was a long way from certainty.

The soldier stopped as if he suddenly remembered himself and who he was in the presence of. He bowed. "My lord, this came from Madame Orcee. She feels an invasion coming."

Cirvel felt his lips tighten. "Of course she would." What distraction did Madame Orcee have up her sleeve now? If he could have his way, he'd have all of the Orcee thrown from the high cliffs and let their bodies rot in the sea. On occasion, though, they did have their purpose.

Besides, he knew the quick way, in this case, to confirm if Madame Orcee's message was true. He looked to Treshauna, who nodded right before she stepped into the shadows.

The soldier was clearly unnerved by Treshauna's disappearance, but Cirvel had more questions. "Did Madame Orcee say what the Death Rogues' intentions are?"

"No, my lord," he answered.

Cirvel sighed. "Bring the speaker of the prophecy to me, and find her sisters to bring as well."

"My lord?"

It was an unusual request, Cirvel knew, but if the Orcee had lied about the prophecy, he wanted to send a swift message back to them. He would not endure lies.

"Have her guide you to the other Orcee in the shop and bring all of them who you find to me. I need at least two Orcee, and try not to bring some poor girl who is merely making her living at the shop," Cirvel said, slowly and forcefully. It wouldn't be an easy request either, but he wanted the soldier to understand just how adamant he was. The Orcee were like rats. You might see one, but another was lurking around somewhere nearby. Cirvel had rarely seen two who were the same and he suspected that their network extended further than he imagined. Chances were good that there were Orcee employed as his servants.

"I will send you back to the tea shop," Cirvel said,

"and, when you have the Orcee gathered, use this to return."

Cirvel pulled his robes away from the tailor as he stepped down from the box to walk toward the soldier. A small version of a magical lamp came to Cirvel's hand. For a moment, he let the lamp turn toward him to pull off a little bit of his sand-like essence, which the genies called duman, before he offered the lamp to the man. "Rub it, and you will return with them to this spot. The duman will surround all of you, so you do not need to touch them."

That brought a small measure of relief to the man's face. Typical teleportation spells of a group of people required touch and some willingness to go. The Orcee wouldn't want to travel together, preferring one only to be seen at a time. But it also would require the soldier to touch the Orcee, something he didn't really want to do any more than he would want to touch Cirvel for fear of being killed for a lack of respect.

Before the soldier could say anything further, Cirvel magically sent him on his way. Cirvel practically felt the soldier land on his feet at the stoop of Madame Orcee's Tea Shop.

But as Cirvel turned to return to the box, halfway through his pivot, he came face to face with a man in a dark cloak – a man he recognized even cloaked -- as scissors tried to pierce Cirvel's gut.

The tailor looked down, shocked that his weapon wasn't piercing flesh.

Were Cirvel any other man, or even any other genie, it would have. But his dragon armor, from the eggshell he'd been incubated in far longer than any other novihomidrak, protected him.

Cirvel's gaze raised from the scissors still pointed toward his stomach though the hands that held them now trembled to the tailor's blue eyes. The Death Rogue wouldn't be going anywhere. Not only was he old, but Death Rogues didn't have the same abilities which Black Nights did to step into the shadows and disappear. It was easy enough for Cirvel to reach out and bind this man's magic.

"You've been playing a long game," Cirvel said, letting his calm voice bring terror to the man's heart. "Remind me, how long have you been my tailor?"

The scissors lowered away from him, but the tailor didn't step back. "Since you conquered Queen Marthryn. I was her tailor before."

"Was there ever any plan to assassinate her, or did you know of my arrival?" Cirvel knew fair well that the Orcee could be behind all this. In fact, chances were good. From the moment he'd arrived on this world, he'd had a natural dislike for the Orcee, and they held him in the same regard. They were testing him right now, and had sent an old, expendable man to do it.

"Milord, how is an old man like me supposed to get any notice? If others were coming, I needed to take the opportunity which my position had suddenly afforded me."

"This was opportunity, not directive?"

The tailor nodded and sent his eyes downcast. He waited for Cirvel to dole out punishment.

"And you were doing so nicely on my robes," Cirvel said with disgust, turning.

The old man's body fell behind him, the tailor's back cracking against the box on which Cirvel had stood. It would have been quite painful if the tailor hadn't already been dead.

Treshauna stepped up beside Cirvel and put her hand on his arm. "I'm sorry he betrayed you, my love."

He refused to look at her, knowing that she would still have the tailor's life energy in her other hand. As a novihomidrak, a Black Night's ability to manipulate, even take, life energy roused his instincts to protect against chaos. As long as he didn't take notice of her work, she wouldn't come up against his dragon aspects.

"I don't know why you would hesitate to kill someone who would clearly harm you. You are a novihomidrak."

Cirvel nodded though he wasn't sure if she was watching him or not. "It is precisely because I'm a novihomidrak. We are champions born from the dragon; we are meant to be helpers guiding life along."

"Oh, my love, are you going to add to the argument between us? I will always maintain that energy standing in the way of what you are accomplishing is better off transformed."

"But you do it more elegantly." He waited a

moment to see if her scoff at words would produce more from her. When it didn't, he continued, "I have only my wits to influence people, and I would prefer to bring their energy to my way of thinking sooner rather than later."

With a deeper laugh, she left his side and walked toward the door of their bedroom. He turned carefully as she went. He would not watch, but his ears would pick up her incantations as she set the energy into the stones of the castle.

"Through doors all lives pass," she said and he knew she was kneeling at the open entrance. "Energy is never created nor destroyed. It only transforms. Set in stone, I seal you. Protect long this castle well."

With that, Cirvel's body calmed, and he could face Treshauna once more.

"Do you think that someday you'll have to fortify the stones to hold in all the energy I'm transferring to them?" she asked.

"It's a large castle," he said, not really wanting to think about the question she posed. He had noticed that many people – humans, particularly sensitive individuals – had begun to comment about feeling watched or that something was moving around them.

"I know that you wish you didn't have to remove threats to our family and our reign in this way, but when it is necessary, this is the best course of action."

Of course, she was right. He only wished that he could make it so she didn't have to. She'd be bored then, as she often told him. Besides, cut off from the Onesong as this world was, someone needed to cleanse the energy. She and Hazem would be the last, unless this world could be forgiven and returned to the Onesong. No matter how deeply he searched his heart, Cirvel didn't believe it could happen. This world deserved no forgiveness.

Yet it was a world he'd promised to serve, so he must do what he could to prolong its survival.

"Did you sense any other threats?" he asked.

"None," she answered, "and only the tailor's as he struck."

"The Orcee will be here soon. I'd prefer to have you in the shadows, hopefully beyond their reach and sight."

She came warmly to his arms, kissed him, and disappeared. So strange that his deepest love also held his broadest fears and elevated anxieties.

"You won't protect her forever," an older female voice said. "She's destined to die. What will you do when that happens, oh self-proclaimed Lord of Gohaldinest."

He felt the energies of the collected Orcee rise up over his back and roll into his neck where the hairs began to stand on end. He fought to control his dragon aspects once more. What was it about these Orcee that raised his ire so quickly? Did they mate with chaos in order to have their visions of the future?

Cirvel pivoted to face the five women and the guard who had brought the Orcee to him.

His thoughts jumped to the tailor's body and what they must be imagining when they saw the corpse on the floor but, when he dared to look, he noticed that there was no body. Treshauna had pulled it into the shadows at some point that he's thankfully not seen. He was really going to miss that tailor. But he knew Treshauna was right: the man had been lying in wait for his opportunity for far too long a time. Why had the tailor chosen this one if he wasn't working with the Orcee?

The women, all of whom were Madame Orcee, showed no relation at all. Some were fair of skin and hair and others dark in their beauty. They were old to young, but not so youthful to be children. They all had power; Cirvel could feel it from them.

He often wondered how the Orcee were found and trained, for it just seemed that one day a new Orcee had appeared in their tea shop. No matter how he'd set people to discover what the Orcee were and how their numbers grew, no information had ever been brought back to him. He'd also never heard of one of their number dying, though he knew that they weren't immortal. It would seem that the Orcee were just as mysterious to him as were their readings. The one thing he knew for certain was that he hated their kind, and yet he'd found them invaluable.

He hoped this meeting wouldn't change his mind.

The women all huddled a little closer together, some taking the hands of others, and fear crept into their eyes. Cirvel wondered how many of them had foreseen this moment. Did they know what was going to happen? That he might get angry enough to rip them to shreds with his claws, and that they'd be unable to stop him as his dragon aspects took over. Or maybe, as Treshauna stood in the shadows, maybe she bound their powers from the darkness, for certainly what the Orcee did had energy behind it. Treshauna loved to remind him that everything was energy. Did that include the source of the Orcee's visions? Did they just read lines of energy which fanned out into possibilities?

"Who breathed life into her vision of Death Rogues by speaking it aloud?" Cirvel asked. When all of the Orcee stiffened and none answered, he continued, "Come now! One of you at least has spoken that Death Rogues from Plenelia infiltrated the castle. One man is now dead over this. If this is a true vision, say it now, tell your Lord of Gohaldinest what you've seen, and let's be done with this."

One of the elder Orcee stepped forward, bringing with her the dank scent of musty age. She was short, and her shoulders had a forward slump to them. Her hands, fingers of wrinkled skin, shook as she pointed an index finger at Cirvel. He could tell that once her eyes would have been shrewd and sharp, but now he doubted that her vision was very good, clouded as her blue eyes were.

"You dishonor us by bringing us as a group. The Orcee only gather in private. It is for our protection, and you have betrayed that. We have no reason now to give you what you want because you threaten us all," she said.

He slapped his hand down on a small dark wood vanity beside him. "I am your lord. I found this vision important enough to have you all brought to me straight away." Extending his arms, he raised his hands, palms up, to indicate the room around them. "Straight to my bedchambers, my most personal of chambers. I do not wish for carnage in this room."

He paused here, then lowered his voice. "It would lead me to needing to find another room in the castle which would displease me greatly. None other have a view quite like that one from the balcony."

As predicted, this evoked nervous twitters from the Orcee. A couple even dared to glance at the balcony as if they could see the view for themselves. Perhaps they did. If they did, hopefully that made them understand.

A dark Orcee released the hands of her sisters and came forward now. Her hair was curly black and formed a pillowy circle around her head. She was not the youngest of the bunch, but she was close, and her palms were nearly flushed pink compared to the rest of her rich umber skin. This day, she'd chosen a light flowing brown skirt and a bulkier sweater of green. He suspected it was over a lighter tunic so that, as the day warmed, she could remove the layer and not become overheated. Around her neck was a simple silver chain adorned with a single daisy flower crafted also in silver.

Cirvel waited for her to speak.

She almost needed to be urged by the others.

"Milord, I am the one who had the vision, though several of us have also seen glimmers. At first, I didn't know what to make of it." She paused here and trembled.

The elder Orcee put her hand on the younger's shoulder, and the dark woman seemed to take comfort in the touch. "She is young and still learning, milord," the older woman said.

"But she said enough that it reached my ears. Tell me, young one, what did you see?" Cirvel asked, moving closer to the group. He very much wanted it to seem like he was looming over them.

The young woman's brown eyes were hardened as she glanced at Cirvel. "That you would gather us here and we would be beset upon. Protect us, milord, as we hold your answer."

The metallic tang of magic around him filled Cirvel's senses. He'd never known any Orcee to actually possess magic, only future-sight. This was not coming from them.

"It's going to rip us apart."

"It wants to know what's in our hearts."

"Milord!"

The choir of voices came at Cirvel like thundering hooves at a chariot race, all driven by fear and anxiety. It overtook him, leaving him tumbling as if he'd been trampled by running horses. The duman took over, and he lost himself in a swirl.

He felt Treshauna take his hand right before it dissolved.

When next he lifted his head from where he lay cheek-down in sand, he was surrounded by the Orcee, each of the women urgently urging him to his feet. He clambered, elbows and knees and feet caught in the cloth of his robes, and he had to move uncomfortably in order to stand. Once he was above the hunched height of the women around him, he saw that they were in some sort of arena. Beyond a solid wall the height of two men tall, the auditorium-style stands were filled with people in black cloaks. They all looked like they were Black Nights, but he knew they were not. These abominations were different. Each one of them had been made, created by the hands of man, the magic of dragons, and the touch of death. Their souls had been nearly completely drained from them, and yet tethered to something immortal. He wondered if Treshauna could find the source, and briefly wished he could ask.

The elder Orcee grabbed Cirvel's arm to get his attention. He barely stayed his dragon aspects as her disquieting grip tightened and she hauled herself using strength over weight to draw herself closer. "It will look into our hearts."

"What will?"

Slowly, a chant started to rise from the crowd. Cirvel didn't understand what they were saying until the Orcee at his side also said the word, "Dek'tae."

"Dek'tae! Dek'tae! Dek'tae!" The gathered Death Rogues above them thumped fists in the air as they shouted the name.

A brunette woman, one of the Orcee, rushed forward toward the elder and tried to break the older woman's grip from Cirvel. Her brown braid slid over her shoulder as she looked around to her sisters. "Milord, we've all seen parts of this battle and how it may play out. Let us guide you and we may all survive."

He'd rather have Treshauna at his back than all these Orcee, but what other choice did he have? He hoped that Treshauna had grabbed onto him and slid into his shadow as he had become duman, that she came with him to this place, and that she remained hidden safely in the shadows waiting for her moment to strike.

But he knew he couldn't count on it. She might still be back in Gohaldinest if she'd been unable to travel along with him to wherever he was now.

"Dek'tae comes," the elder Orcee said.

"You will protect us, milord?" the black haired Orcee asked as she came to help the brunette draw the older woman away from him.

He didn't like their kind. They unnerved him.

Whatever this Dek'tae was, he doubted it could hurt him. He was novihomidrak and genie. Not much could bring him harm. But they were afraid of being ripped apart. They'd seen it happen in their visions and knew he had a choice that left them at his mercy.

There was no thrill of triumph here though. These women needed him. The Death Rogues hadn't come for Cirvel, but for the Orcee. One of their number had betrayed them. There were five of them here. He'd never expected his guard to find so many together. Cirvel would have been glad if the guard had brought back two. But there were five.

Four had spoken.

Which meant the one who had hung back had betrayed the others.

He met her calculating green eyes. A redhead with fire in her, through and through. He saw hatred, not only of him but of the others. She was a killer among them and had used her own powers to keep the others from seeing her deceptions.

Cirvel wished he had a way to communicate that with Treshauna. He still didn't know if she was here and, if she was, how deeply in the shadows she was. He knew shadows could be deep and sound might not penetrate. It was always risky.

The sand beneath their feet heaved. Orcee were knocked around.

Even Red looked a little scared, and that worried Cirvel. If this was her plan, surely she had a way out.

Unless she didn't know what Dek'tae was either.

Maybe a Death Rogue had slipped information to her ... just enough to tantalize into this plan, but not enough to actually save herself. Oh, she could be in trouble too.

A dark tentacle rose from the sand and flailed around in the air. It glistened as if it had been underwater, but had no sand sticking to it as it would if it were wet.

The sight of the tentacle brought a roar from the crowd. Several of those in the stands stood up and thrust both hands in the air as if claiming victory.

Even the Orcee were picking up on the fact that the crowd was out for blood, and they quickly huddled and moved away from the lump in the sand where the tentacle rose.

The dark Orcee grabbed Cirvel's arm. "We've seen the battle. You must listen to us."

"You've been lied to. One of you set this up." He pulled his clothes out of her grip. If she dared to ask who, he'd tell her that she was the one with visions and should be able to figure it out. But she didn't, and he moved away from her.

He tipped his head toward the sand, wanting neither Orcee nor the audience to hear him. "Treshauna, if you can hear me, get them out of here."

It was time to find out what Dek'tae was.

He grabbed onto the tentacle which flailed in the air, but the moment it had contact, it seemed to know that he was the prey and shot up four more tentacles from the sand. Two surrounded him while the first twisted in his grip to take a tight hold onto him. The fourth tentacle missed him completely until it rounded back. Smart creature. It had gauged his size.

The Orcee were still here, inching further away as the tentacles secured Cirvel. Treshauna hadn't heard him, or she couldn't reach him at his location – wherever that was. This was not part of the castle he knew. He'd explored it all, including the dungeons and the huge auditorium not too unlike this, where a dragon had once been held as entertainment. Here, he didn't feel the echoes of the dragon's pain as it screamed across the Humline. Here, he barely felt the Humline. It was almost like this arena was an echo of the one in his castle.

If that were true, this could be a chaos monster.

The quickly cutting thoughts speeding through his mind to make sense of the situation were cut short by the creature hauling him into the air and pulling his arms and legs out.

The Orcee beneath him shrieked and gasped behind hands covering their mouths.

The tentacles massaged his muscles and bones and they tightened their grip around his wrists and ankles. *"What pains you in your heart?"*

The voice rattled deep within Cirvel's head and lived like an echo there worming its way into places he had no idea existed within him.

Lots of things. He felt the reply sing from his heart before he'd even thought about the words. "I'm a novihomidrak," he whispered, knowing that of all things, that truth brought him the most pain. Glory, but pain. Being a unique novihomidrak made it doubly so.

"*Tell me,*" it said, rippling, tightening, begging.

Cirvel felt his muscles stretching uncomfortably. He saw the crowd chanting for Dek'tae and cheering the creature on, but he no longer heard them. From the corner of his eye, he saw the Orcee looking for a way out. They wanted to flee.

And he'd been having such a nice morning!

That was pain too. He'd woken in a good mood, opened his balcony doors to fantastic morning light, drank tea, and watched Treshauna sleep as he waited for the tailor – that dreadful, treacherous tailor – to show up and continue the fitting for the new robes he was designing for his kingdom.

Now, he had to end this creature, and the Death Rogues gathered in the stands, all before he'd had his breakfast. And! And he didn't even know why they were doing this.

"*And...?*" the creature urged him to continue.

Interesting. Cirvel felt the creature, this Dek'tae whatever it was, sliding like a poison through his veins. It went straight to the heart, seized the emotions, and drew them out as one might bite into a juicy pear. He thought of Treshauna eating the fruit this morning shortly after it had arrived.

One day, she would no longer live in this world. How would he be without her? How would he survive? Oh, that... that right there... good pain.

Cirvel felt his heart beating faster now. It was betraying him.

His children, his beautiful children – Kahlila who looked like her mother but had his magic, and Hazem who bore Cirvel's dark look but carried Treshauna's abilities –would someday leave this world too. Even though they might have lives longer than normal humans, they were cursed with mortality. Being three-quarters human, they wouldn't even make it into the long years that an ordinary half-genie would have. Cycles on this world. Cirvel had to remember that. This planet had a strange orbit, one that could only be explained by a dragon's pain – and hatred of what he'd created enough that he wanted to destroy it – mixed in with a lingering love and the fear of loss.

Oh, how Cirvel understood.

This whole world could die ... and Cirvel would remain.

He was unique. Did that mean he was also destined to eventually be alone? A novihomidrak trapped in a world cut off from the rest of the universe? Would he be forced to someday use his own weapons on himself to end his misery when loneliness from a solitary existence seemed too much to bear? How long could he stand being away from the Onesong before madness crept in?

For so long, he'd held his emotions in. Genies always held themselves in check, and he doubly so because of his weaker human half. Then, to be a novihomidrak. It all felt so heavy and tight within his chest. If this is what was meant by *soul-crushing*, he understood it now.

"*Do go on...*" Dek'tae invited.

Cirvel knew he could. His mindset could unravel out of control. This creature would love every second of it. If he were honest, he might too. To go down that long dark rabbit hole of self-loathing. It would, as people say, be a slippery slope that he'd not easily recover from. He already felt himself there, beginning the fall.

Cirvel. Treshauna whispered in his mind. For whatever reason, it made him raise his gaze, and he saw one of the Death Rogues stand. Except he saw the face beneath the cloak, the face of the woman he loved. Other Death Rogues followed suit as if they were giving him a standing ovation, or were prepared to cheer as Dek'tae ripped him apart.

He felt the stress of Dek'tae's tentacles pulling at his limbs. Novihomidraks could be injured, even have joints dislocated. Injuries for him came with the added complication that his long incubation inside his dragon mother had set a fine layer of venomcur beneath his skin, something that typically only novihomidraks of Ch'bauldi dragons had. This would only be a threat if somehow Dek'tae did manage to tear him apart. A little part – a wildly curious part – of his mind wanted to know if it could be done.

But not in front of Treshauna. Not to give these Death Rogues from Plenelia the joy they sought. There they stood like they were all Black Nights looking down on him. He wouldn't admit it to Treshauna, but he knew that somewhere in those deep recesses of his mind he still held an animosity toward the Black Nights for bringing him to this forsaken world. He may have forsaken the allegiance he wanted to the dragon Alexander in order to serve Leschemal, but he hadn't forgotten. He sure hadn't forgiven either.

But the only Black Nights who would ever be on this world were Drelin, now dead, Treshauna, who had come to this world with Cirvel and Drelin, and Hazem, born as a direct descendant of Treshauna. It had been due to Cirvel's genie magic that had given Hazem the abilities of a Black Night. Cirvel and Treshauna doubted such fortune would occur again.

Be damned this Dek'tae for allowing his thoughts to stray even as it tugged and strained while calling out in his mind for him to continue. It was slowly getting Cirvel to reveal everything about his life, his love, and all his fears. This Dek'tae roamed his mind, tiptoed around to take peeks at what scared Cirvel about the future while it sought around in the past to find the motivations behind those terrors. Here would be a creature that would understand Cirvel possibly better than he knew himself because it would have the objectivity of its own distant brain.

What a creature this could be! What Cirvel could accomplish if he knew what lay in the hearts of the people around him. Of the Orcee. Of the tailor who had died almost needlessly because he'd taken an opportunity. If Cirvel had known, could he have saved the tailor?

A tentacle slid up around Cirvel's neck, and he tugged his arm down, fighting against Dek'tae's restraining hold, just in time to keep Dek'tae from getting a strangle hold. It left him tangling painfully by one arm, but if he could keep his airway open, it would be worth it. Novihomidraks could be knocked unconscious too. At least he had little worry about a sleeping death, where a novihomidrak drowned or suffocated but never actually died, but he never wanted to figure out if he could have such an experience.

"You don't easily come apart," Dek'tae said in his mind. *"Humans usually beg me to tear them to pieces by now."*

"I am no human, not completely, and maybe not even that anymore," Cirvel said.

Cirvel, come on, get away from that creature, Treshauna said in his mind.

Not now, darling, he said back. *Negotiations have just begun.*

He didn't know if Dek'tae could hear his internal

conversation with Treshauna or not but, if it could, he didn't mind letting on that he was willing to bargain.

"*What are you if not human? You look human,*" Dek'tae said.

One of Dek'tae's tentacles had slid between his arm and his throat. The tentacles were pure muscle.

Cirvel called his magical lamp to hand. It banged against his face as the tentacle trying to circle his neck rippled along. He tried turning it in his fingers so that it wasn't hitting him, but he was afraid to drop it. If he did, and one of Dek'tae's tentacles happened by sheer luck to catch it, it might be considered by some a transfer in the possession of the lamp. Cirvel wasn't ready to take that chance.

"Rub the lamp, Dek'tae," Cirvel said, "and find out what I am."

One of those strong tentacles reached by Cirvel's face, knocking uncomfortably against his nose. He turned his head aside.

He thought he heard the Orcee shouting at him. Maybe they were telling him what to do. They'd claimed to know how he won, how he lost, but his ears were filled with pressure, and he couldn't make out any of what they said.

One did not want to go casually into battle with a novihomidrak though. Most novies, if they saw things turning sour, would walk away. Novies had missions.

His mission was to save Leschemal's world.

Once again, the Death Rogues filled his view as the

lamp nearly twisted from his fingers. Dek'tae was rubbing it, possibly trying to decide if it were living or not.

But it was enough.

Cirvel turned to duman and let himself be pulled into the lamp. Now it was his turn to wrap around Dek'tae and spin the creature into duman. He heard it shriek in his mind, and Cirvel delighted in the way he took it apart.

He surged into the lamp and, still as a smokey cloud, whipped through the interior out to the sands beyond the house within his lamp. There he brought Dek'tae back before he landed his own feet on the ground outside the distance of the tentacles.

While the creature had dark extremities, the mass of its body was clear, and Cirvel observed several throbbing organs within. They weren't the normal body systems that most living beings had. It seemed to have no mouth and no digestive system, but it did have eyes, about twenty or so all on small wobbling stems near the top of its body where it seemed logical to call it a head, and yet it wasn't. It was more like the top of the mass. There appeared to be no ears either.

Dek'tae huffed – as if its whole body was taking in air – and it inflated. It hoisted itself up on several tenta-cles. The desert sun seemed to go right through it, only tinting the brownish-yellow sand beneath with the slightest of shadow. It grew until it stood taller than Cirvel and it rotated to look down at Cirvel.

"All of them."

"And those who come afterward. I will have a very long life, my friend, and, as I said, I will have many enemies over the course of that time. I will also be gathering new people to my side. Humans have short lives, you know. I will need people tested on a near continuous basis."

Dek'tae was shaking by the time Cirvel finished. It all seemed too good to be true. A feast of emotions for a long time.

"Those humans will not bend to you easily. They do not perish willingly."

"Clearly you do not need to live in sand and you are capable of movement." Cirvel was glad he'd taken the chance to bring Dek'tae here to his genie home to learn about the creature. It had afforded them a precious moment.

"Hiding in sand. They never know when I will strike."

"Dek'tae, you are a fearsome creature in sight and doing. No one likes their darkest secrets revealed. The sight of you would terrify common mortals. These Death Rogues will come to love your touch. None will want to be put in the arena with you, but everyone will want to watch." Cirvel saw the whole thing playing out in his mind as if he had the future-sight of the Orcee. Had they suspected this? They couldn't always see him properly in their visions.

Oh, those tricky Orcee. It had never been a battle

with Dek'tae that they saw. They saw the battle with the Death Rogues.

And they weren't necessarily on Cirvel's side.

Right now, they could be informing the Death Rogues of what they did see of Cirvel's plan. Did they know that he'd be bringing Dek'tae back as an ally? Had the Orcee seen this as their moment to get rid of Cirvel? Had the Death Rogues come to them, wanting to find a way to kill Dek'tae, and this plot had been hatched? Cirvel knew he was going to have to do some despicable things in order to save Leschemal's world. He accepted this. He knew he'd create his enemies. He knew attempts would be made against his life. None of that he feared for himself.

But Treshauna, she was with the Orcee and the Death Rogues right now.

Feeling his heartbeat quicken, he forced himself to remember that she was a Black Night and plenty capable of taking care of herself. She would not go down easily. For that matter, she'd slip to the shadows and they'd never find her. He must believe that she'd be perfectly safe, or he'd rush in and do something fool-ish. He'd done that before.

Every time he forgot what Treshauna was – and what she could do – she laughed at him. He could practically feel her laughing at him now. Her foolish love.

Oh, they were foolish to love each other. What a tragically doomed relationship.

"Yes...."

Cirvel tightened his arm and half made to pull away, but he realized he'd lose communication with Dek'tae, so he held his hand. "Don't do that. Not to me. Am I being understood?"

"Habit. It's hard. Especially since you are so... saturated with emotion."

"You will get your fill, my friend. I promise you that. But not from me."

Dek'tae's body lowered a little, again with an inaudible sigh. *"Understand. Our touch be for communication."*

"Good."

"But if you break your word, I will come for you and I will make you a living husk."

Cirvel had no doubt that the creature meant what it said, but he did have issues with the fear that recoiled through his stomach. "Understood."

"Good."

"I believe, my friend, that we are equally matched. Let us return to the playing field that was meant for us to compare our skills on and give game to those who wanted to be spectators of our sport."

"They will all follow you, and it will be my pleasure to make them see that this is the better course of action."

Cirvel pulled away before Dek'tae could feed on his next thoughts and emotions. He didn't know how Dek'tae planned on making that happen and he really didn't care. He had plans of his own. Just knowing that they'd be working together was enough. Get through the moment and to the next.

He turned them to duman and returned to the arena via the magical lamp. It didn't surprise Cirvel to see Treshauna now standing in the stadium holding his lamp. As he spilled like smoke from the spout, she raised it higher away from her body as they had often discussed between them. It was a necessary safeguard to protect her from whatever might be coming through the lamp with him. The pose made her look powerful and beautiful as if she were in charge of the emerging genie. There were times like this when there was little doubt that she was his master.

As duman, Cirvel continued into the stands with Dek'tae and let the creature's duman spread among them all before he whipped around and took form beside Treshauna.

"Bind the Death Rogues where they stand," he said, tilting his head toward his wife and speaking low enough for only her ears. When she nodded, she took a step back and his lamp dropped into his hands. She was gone in that instant as he fastened the lamp to his belt. They were so perfect together.

It wasn't as if they hadn't practiced this, but they just knew each other so well. He loved her so much.

The Orcee, on the other hand, he had full view of now that Treshauna had returned to the shadows, and he held a particular dislike of them. As a group, they stepped back as if they all understood their choreography in this moment. The second dance had begun, and it started with Death Rogues screaming.

The gaze of all the Orcee flinched to the stands. Mouths fell open as if they were expecting blood and death in the seats above the sandy arena. Had they seen it in some of their visions?

What would it be like to have the visions and to see them coming alive before the eyes that held those sights?

"Madame Orcee," he said, addressing the group as he took form in front of them. "You have seen the outcome of this battle. What do I do to you?"

"My lord, we are naught but faithful to you," said the eldest Orcee. "Did we not tell you that the Death Rogues were coming for you?"

"You did not. You let rumors come to my ears first. My dear ladies, I find your abilities disturbing and useful." Cirvel paused as another Death Rogue began screaming in such a pitch that Cirvel couldn't speak over it. Once it died away, he continued, "From here on out, you will be faithful to me. You will come willingly when I call, less I turn you over to Dek'tae."

Cirvel turned to look up in the arena stands where Death Rogues were trying to get away from the monster that attacked them. The smart ones were frozen in their fear. Others were not so lucky. Dek'tae seemed to have tentacles for them all.

"That's a very interesting creature you have introduced me to," Cirvel said, grinning. "I don't think we'll be having any more trouble from the Plenelian Death Rogues."

Cirvel looked around for Treshauna. When he did not find her, he merely called out, "My love," and she was standing before him in his next heartbeat. "Would you be so kind as to return the Madames to their tea shop while I finish up here?"

"Their energy will be unbound," she said, tipping her head toward the Death Rogues.

"I think they've had enough, and Dek'tae holds enough of them."

"Ooh, Dek'tae. I can't wait to hear more about him," she said.

He knew he'd have to deal with her curiosity, but he never intended on her knowing the full extent of what Dek'tae could do. Or what Dek'tae had learned about him. All in time.

Cirvel wrapped the Orcee up as duman and tucked them in a bubble inside the lamp, which he then handed to Treshauna. She'd release the Orcee when she got to the tea shop. As she took the lamp he handed to her, she reached up to touch his face with her free hand. He leaned over, cupping her cheek with his own palm, and kissed her.

He still had the feeling of her on his mouth when she stepped into the shadows.

Now that the women were gone ...

The Death Rogues, or some of them, found their

energy free and they tried to flee from the stands. But Cirvel was there standing in their way.

"Everyone stop," Cirvel said. "Dek'tae, release the minds of those you hold."

Silence fell likc a shock around Cirvel. It was like someone had dropped an ocean of cold water on everyone in the arena. Yet Cirvel waited as he saw awareness reach their eyes once more, and their attention focused on him.

"Death Rogues, once of Plenelia, I give you a choice. You may submit to Dek'tae or you can follow my command now. Decide." They would all submit to Dek'tae in time, but they didn't need to know that now.

A Death Rogue with a tentacle wrapped firmly around his neck was the first to speak as he tried to disengage from Dek'tae's appendage. "Milord Cirvel, I am yours to command."

It was the start of a chorus of others in agreement and the disdain of others who would not forsake their country. It was quickly easy to see the dividing line, and more came to Cirvel than got left behind for Dek'tae.

And Dek'tae was quick to sort those who would still stand against Cirvel and make them regret their choices.

He wrapped the Death Rogues choosing him in duman and took them down the sandy arena to watch the coming deaths of those remaining in the stands. Cirvel let the others watch the savagery so that their decision was fully set in their heads as the correct choice.

When he could no longer stomach the horrors himself, he turned to his Death Rogues. "My first order is that no Death Rogue of mine will wear black. From now on, you wear deep purple, the red and blue of human blood ..." Cirvel pointed to the stands. "... their blood. You could not stand with your brethren. You betrayed them and your country to save your lives. That shall never be forgotten, and you shall forever be cloaked in purple."

At once, their robes changed in color by Cirvel's magic. In his spell, he had woven in the very blood he spoke about, blood that would turn to red if any one of them ever betrayed him.

He had so very much to learn about these Death Rogues, and expected there would be disloyalty from at least a few as he satisfied his curiosity about them and how to make more.

Again, time. He was glad he had lots of it.

"How is it that you come by here?" he asked.

"There's a doorway and a spell," one was quick to respond.

That made the most sense.

"Your name?" Cirvel asked the one who had spoken. He was near completely certain this Death Rogue had also been the first to join with him, and there was no better time to start gaining trust than right now.

"Bradson, milord," he said.

"Lead the way, Bradson."

Bradson started, Cirvel followed. Each step made Cirvel wonder if any of those behind him were contemplating using a weapon to run Cirvel through. How many might plot against him and think this might be their first chance? Let them try. Let them discover their new lord wasn't easy to defeat.

But no one made the attempt, and Cirvel was a little disappointed about that. It would have been nice to turn an extra two or three over to Dek'tae as an example to the others.

"Do you have a name for this place?" he thought to ask Bradson.

"Nay, milord. We just call it the arena."

"'Tis important that places have names," Cirvel said as he looked around to the Death Rogues following him. "Much like the importance of names and titles for the living, don't you agree?"

Cirvel saw the nodding of many hoods as there were murmurs of hesitant agreeance. None of them trusted him, so they weren't sure where he was going with this. "From now on, this is The Playground. This is where you will come and train. I will make it a safe space for anyone wearing my honored purple robes. Do not mistake me in this. You will be my elite guards called Necroathelings. Due to your coming, there will be a hierarchy, and you will stand above others. Much as your new title suggests, you will be my dark princes."

He paused for effect here, knowing each one would need a moment to let his words fully sink in that he was fully opening his door to trusting them. He hoped they would walk through it and reciprocate.

When he felt he'd allowed for enough time, he said, "Befitting as such, you will all carry the designation *-na* after your names as a shortened form of Necroatheling. For example, Bradson is now Bradson-na. Congratulations, my dark princes, particularly you, Bradson-na."

The young man flushed, and Cirvel saw just how truly young the boy was. It would take a despicable person, just as Cirvel knew the Lord of Plenelian to be, to push this youth into battle against someone like him.

Maybe it was time to send the Plenelian lord another message that Gohaldinest was not to be trifled with.

But Cirvel realized that the short, dark hallway of stone had stopped at a door where they now all stood.

"What is on the other side of this door?" Cirvel asked.

"The Plenelian castle, milord," Bradson-na responded.

Perhaps Treshauna was right about energy always appearing at the correct time. Strange that he would think about sending the Lord of Plenelia a message at the moment he arrived at a doorway that would step him directly into Lord Sydren's castle.

He turned a bright smile to the Necroathelings. "Well, we'll just have to change that, won't we? But first, would anyone like to say good-bye to their former sovereign?"

There was definite hesitation now, and Cirvel was pretty sure most of them were thinking that Cirvel would kill them right in front of the lord as a means of sending a message.

"Bradson-na, please lower your hood," Cirvel said.

Bradson-na raised his hands, paused, then with shaking fingers pushed back the hood of the now purple cloak. He trembled as he slid a questioning look to Cirvel.

"I do not know what each of you has endured to become a Death Rogue," Cirvel said, "but I know that, from what I feel, each has undergone a powerful trans-formation using unholy magicks. That is what Lord Sydren does. He once sought to imprison me. He intended on using me up, much as he now will take a boy from wherever he came from and use him up as a Death Rogue. I guarantee that he set you all against me, figuring that none of you would survive. He expected you all to be lost. If any of you did return, then that would be a boon, as he'd get information about the battle with me and how the others lost. Does that sound fair to you?"

Several of the Necroathelings glanced around, validating Cirvel's words with their friends. The confirming nods started slowly but strengthened as they all began to agree.

Bradson-na turned to Cirvel. "He takes all of us from our families." Bradson-na's voice was low so that only Cirvel could hear. "There are many of our families taken before us, and we don't know what happens to them. We never find out, but we have to assume that they died."

Cirvel placed a hand on Bradson-na's shoulder. "That is the kind of man your lord is. Rest assured that – going forward – anyone who chooses to be a Necroatheling will be doing it from their own choice, not mine, and the rewards will be great."

He pulled his hand away from Bradson-na and lowered it slowly as he gazed out over the others. "Best yet, you all are my founder Necroathelings. You are here now by your choice, not by command."

There was a slim line of truth there, and he knew it. He waited in case anyone wanted to call him out on it. They didn't. In fact, a cheer rose. Cirvel's heart elated at the sound. He doubted any of them would betray him now.

There was no need to go taunt this in front of Lord Sydren. He would assume that all his Death Rogues had been lost. Someday, probably soon, one of their number would get a letter outside of Gohaldinest either to Sydren or to kin, and that would inform the people of Plenelia that those Sydren had sent had turned against him to follow Cirvel. That would be enough.

How many wives and children would be coming up the mountain to live in Gohaldinest? Cirvel would have to open the gates to admit them. Necroathelings deserved rewards, after all, and family was a fantastic reward. In a couple of generations, Plenelian blood would begin mixing with those whose families had lived in Gohaldinest for as many generations as they could remember. New blood was also good.

A Death Rogue invasion. Had the Orcee's vision seen this? Was that why the prophecy had been vague with them believing that Death Rogues were in the castle?

Perhaps the Orcee were not as strong as they wished to be.

After all, they had clearly missed the one Death Rogue who always had a pair of scissors and several needles every time he came around Cirvel. Clearly, they weren't as powerful as they thought themselves.

Cirvel found the spell at the edge of the door and unanchored it from Plenelia. No one disturbed him while he did this. The Necroathelings all seemed ready to have it done.

He reattached it to a long staircase in Gohaldinest and gave a bit of confusion to the spell to disorientate those coming through. Since he didn't want anyone coming upon Dek'tae by accident, he added a word to activate the door and a lion head knocker to awaken the spell.

There would be a lot to get done once he had the Necroathelings back in Gohaldinest. Orientation, housing, discussions with his current guards, learning how Death Rogues were created, and on and on. Cirvel felt his list growing.

He pushed all his worries and tasks back and turned, smiling, once more to the first group of people he was welcoming to Gohaldinest. "Are you ready to go home?"

The Necroathelings gave not quite cheers this time, but affirmations of their readiness. Bradson-na stepped forward. "We're ready, Lord Cirvel."

The Orcee's vision was about to become true.

Cirvel opened the door, and, just like that, Necroathelings were at home in the castle at Gohaldinest.

A genie champion who wants to serve
an imagination dragon.
All that changes when a beautiful
woman steals his lamp.

THE FATE OF THE WORLD LIES IN HIS HANDS. BUT IS HE THE REDEEMER OR SOMETHING FAR WORSE?

PRAISE FOR TANGLED MAGIC:

"I highly recommend reading all of Ms. Blair's tales as she is masterfully crafting many universes to explore."

WWW.MORNINGSKYSTUDIOS.COM

No one believed the warning. Only she heard the stones screaming.

WWW.MORNINGSKYSTUDIOS.COM

Ready for another quest?

Sign up for Dawn Blair's newsletter to learn about new releases, hear about events, and more!

It's easy.

Go to **www.dawnblair.com/newsletter** to join the adventure.

Dawn Blair grew up on a ranch in a rural Nevada town. The many old buildings on the property provided inspiration for her imagination as she thrived on stories of unicorns, princesses, heroic knights, and hidden doors to other dimensions.

For as long as she can remember, Dawn has had a passion for storytelling. She loves creating worlds and spinning tales for people to enjoy. The best ones are the stories that surprise her as she's writing.

Her creativity has also spread out into painting, drawing, and audiobook narration.

Thank you for taking the time to join her on these adventures.

Find more about Dawn and her work at:
www.morningskystudios.com

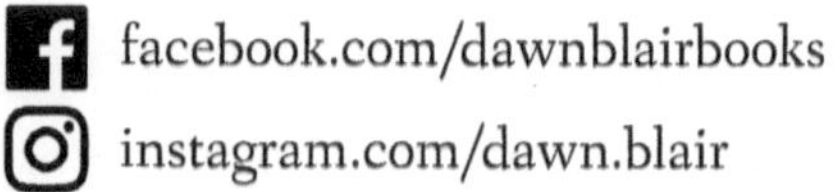